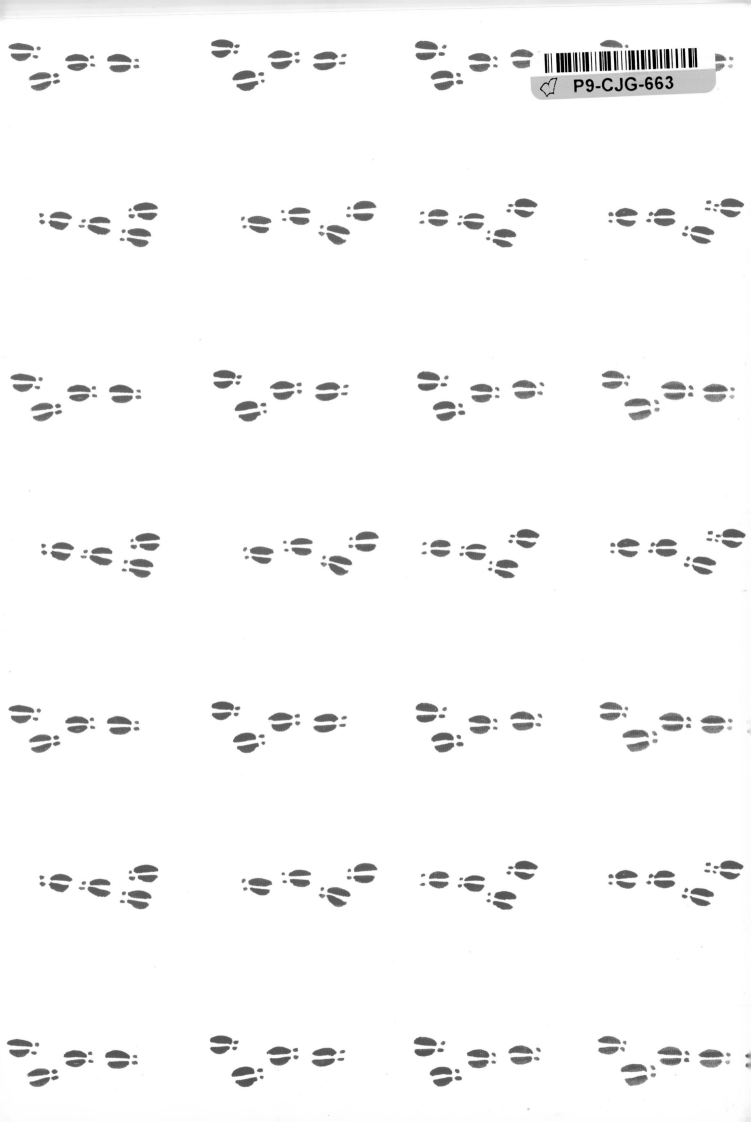

Translated by Tara Chace.

Text and illustrations copyright © 1985 by Sven Nordqvist.
This edition published in Sweden by Bokförlaget Opal AB under the title *Pannkakstårtan*.
English translation copyright © 2015 by NorthSouth Books Inc., New York 10016.

First published in the United States and Canada in 2015 by NorthSouth Books Inc.,
an imprint of NordSüd Verlag AG, CH-8005, Zürich, Switzerland.

Distributed in the United States by NorthSouth Books Inc., New York 10016.
Library of Congress Cataloging-in-Publication Data is available.

ISBN: 978-0-7358-4203-8
Printed at Livonia Print, Latvia.
1 3 5 7 9 • 10 8 6 4 2
www.northsouth.com

The Adventures of Pettson and Findus

The Birthday Cake

Sven Nordqvist

North
South

Once upon a time there was an old man named Pettson. He had a cat named Findus. Together they lived in a little red house with a toolshed, a chicken coop, a woodshed, an outhouse, and a garden—surrounded by fields and meadows.

People said Pettson was crazy. But people say so many things, you never know what to believe. True, sometimes Pettson was a little forgetful, and he often walked around alone talking to his cat. Those things wouldn't have seemed so bad if it wasn't for what Mr. Gustavsson told everyone about Pettson's pancake mix. And how he climbed over the roof to get to the store. And how he tied a curtain onto his cat's tail. Gustavsson saw it with his own eyes, so it had to be true. If a man acted like that, he had to be crazy, right?

It all happened on Findus's birthday. Findus had three birthdays a year just because it was more fun that way. Every time the cat had a birthday, Pettson made him a birthday cake out of pancakes and whipped cream.

That morning Pettson had been in the chicken coop gathering eggs. Then he sat on the bench outside while he polished them. They had to be good and clean because Pettson liked to do things properly. Findus paced impatiently back and forth on the bench, waiting for the pancake making to begin.

"Do you really need to clean all the eggs NOW?" the cat asked, irritated.
"I'll have another whole birthday before this cake is done."

"You're so impatient," said the old man. "Well, I suppose we can take
three eggs into the kitchen and see if there'll be a cake."

"Of course there'll be a cake," said Findus. He was already in the kitchen
looking for the skillet. They left the rest of the eggs outside in the basket on
the bench.

Pettson cracked the eggs into a bowl.

"Now we need milk, sugar, a little salt, butter, and flour," he said, selecting the ingredients from the pantry. But he couldn't find the flour.

"Where's the flour? Findus, did you eat all the flour?" he called from the pantry.

"I most certainly did not eat any flour," Findus said indignantly.

"Then I guess I must have done it myself," muttered the old man, scratching his nose pensively.

He searched the whole pantry three more times, along with the woodstove, the closet, and the kitchen bench; but he didn't find any flour.

"I guess I'll have to bike to the store and buy some more flour. You wait here," Pettson told the cat.

But the cat didn't want to wait there, so he rushed outside ahead of Pettson.

But when Pettson went to get on his bike, he noticed that his back tire was flat.

"What's this? Findus, did you bite a hole in my tire?" the old man grumbled, a little annoyed.

"I most certainly did not bite any hole in any tire," the cat replied indignantly.

"Then I guess I must have done it myself," mumbled the old man, tugging on his ear. "You wait here, and I'll go get a couple of tools from the shed. Then I'll fix the flat and go buy some flour, and then we can make your birthday cake."

But the cat didn't want to just sit there, so he ran ahead to the shed.

But when Pettson went to open the
shed door, the key was missing and
the door wouldn't open.

"What's going on here?" the old man
grumbled. "This door is never locked.
Findus, did you lose the key?"

"I most certainly did not lose any key,"
the cat said, completely indignant.

"Then I guess I must have done it
myself. What a nuisance," grumbled the
old man, rubbing his eye.

Then Findus whistled from the well, pointing down. Pettson hurried over.

"Would you look at that? There's the key, all the way down at the bottom. How did it get there? And how am I going to get it out?" He tugged at his lip and thought for a long time before he suddenly leaped up. "I know! If I put a hook on a long stick, I could use that to fish out the key. Findus, do you have a long stick?"

"I most certainly have never had a long stick," said Findus, unsure whether he should be indignant.

"Well, I guess I must have one somewhere then," grumbled the old man, scratching at his hat. "You wait here, and I'll go find one. Then I can fish out the key, so I can fetch the tools and fix the bicycle, so I can go buy more flour, so we can get back to making your cake."

But the cat didn't want to wait there, so he ran off ahead to look for sticks.

Pettson and his cat looked all over the place for a long stick. They looked in the chicken coop, behind the shed, in the garden, behind the formal sofa, and in the pantry. But they didn't find a long stick anywhere until it occurred to Pettson that he had a long fishing rod in the attic over the shed.

The fishing rod will work, thought Pettson. Just have to get the ladder, climb over the roof, and go in through the skylight. But the ladder is behind Andersson's woodshed, and Andersson's angry bull is using the ladder as a pillow. So I don't dare go get it, because the bull will wake up and go nuts. We'll have to lure him away somehow. Now, how are we going to do that? Pettson thought so hard you could hear his brain buzzing.

After pondering the situation for a long time, the old man asked Findus,
"Are you a good bullfighter?"

"I've never fought a single bull before," Findus said, frightened.

"Too bad," Pettson said worriedly. "Because if we can't lure the bull away then I can't get the ladder and then I can't get the fishing rod and then I can't fish the key out of the well and then I can't fix the bicycle and then I can't go buy more flour and then there won't be any birthday cake. And what kind of a birthday will it be if we don't have any cake?"

Findus sat in silence for a bit and then said, "Well, of course I've made the odd cow or two run, so I could probably get that old bull moving in a pinch."

"I thought as much . . . if your birthday cake was depending on it," Pettson said, winking at the cat. "Even the fastest cat in the world can be a little lazy sometimes. You just wait here," he said, walking into the house.

The old man fetched a curtain from the kitchen, his gramophone, and a record, then went outside and tied the curtain onto the cat's tail.

"Matadors in Spain use a curtain like this when they fight bulls," Pettson said. "Now, don't start running until I say Go!" Then Pettson placed the gramophone next to the fence where Andersson's bull was sleeping and wound it up. A famous opera singer—another old man— started singing "To the Sea." "This would wake anyone up," Pettson said, chuckling with delight.

At first the song was quiet; the singer was holding back. But when the singer gave it his all, the song exploded! The bull jumped straight up in the air and looked around in alarm.

What was that? the bull wondered. Then he spun around and spotted Pettson, the cat, and the gramophone. "Stop that noise or I'll do it myself!" he grunted.

And he lowered his head, tensed all his muscles, and took off running in a burst of speed straight toward Pettson, Findus, and the gramophone.

"Go!" Pettson whispered to the cat. "Run as fast as you can!"

Findus darted off like a comet with the yellow-and-red floral curtain fluttering from his tail. When the bull spotted that, he turned sharply and tore after it.

When they were halfway across the pasture,
Pettson hurriedly scrambled through the fence.
He quickly grabbed the ladder and snuck back
out as Findus returned at record speed with his
yellow-curtain tail behind him.

The bull, who was panting at the far end of
the meadow, wondered what had happened.

Findus on the other hand kept going, propelled by sheer speed, past the bench where the basket of eggs was sitting. The curtain snagged the basket, tipping it over so the eggs fell out and broke into a puddle. A moment later Pettson also got tangled in the curtain, tripping and landing on his bottom in the middle of the gloppy mess. Not a single egg was left unbroken.

Pettson let out a stream of bad words then scrambled to his feet, glaring at the gooey puddle.

"Findus, why did you leave the egg basket on the bench? Now look at it!" he fussed.

"I most certainly did not leave any eggs on any benches!" the cat hissed indignantly.

"I guess I must have done it then!" the old man hissed back. Then he calmed down again, since it was Findus's birthday.

"This is terrible." He sighed. "I'm going to have to do some cleaning before I can get back to work on your birthday cake, because I'm the sort of old man who likes to do things properly."

He got a shovel and started scooping the muddy egg mixture into a tin bucket. And that's when Gustavsson showed up.

"Hello, Pettson! Working hard as usual, I see," said Gustavsson, eyeing the eggy mess with curiosity.

"We're celebrating a birthday, you know, so I'm making the pancake batter. I'm going to make us a really nice birthday cake," said Pettson, scooping up the last shovel full of egg mud from the puddle.

Then Pettson realized that his pants were all eggy and muddy. *I suppose I could treat myself to a new pair of pants. After all, this pair is more than thirty years old*, he thought, taking off the pants.

"Might as well toss these in, too. If you only have a birthday three times a year, you might as well celebrate in style," he said, stuffing his pants into the bucket.

Gustavsson just stared at the mess in the tin bucket. Pancake batter?! He glanced over at Pettson uneasily. The old man must have totally lost it. The best thing to do was probably to pretend everything was normal.

"I see. A pancake birthday cake for you and the cat . . . sounds nice!" Gustavsson said, trying to sound encouraging.

"Yessirree, my own recipe," Pettson said proudly. "But first we have to go to the store and buy some flour. Wait here a while and I'll be back."

Then Pettson took the ladder, walked over to his shed, climbed up onto the roof, and disappeared somewhere on the far side.

Gustavsson stood there for a few seconds, peering up at the roof. Then he looked down at the muddy egg slop in the bucket and at the cat, who was pacing impatiently back and forth with a yellow-and-red floral curtain tied to his tail, and at the wind-up gramophone, which was stuck and kept screeching, *"To the seeea, to the seeea, to the seeea."*

Then Gustavsson looked back up at the roof, where Pettson had disappeared. "Um, the store is in the other direction," he said in a quiet voice. Then he turned around and went home. He looked as if he was deep in thought.

From that day on, everyone in town thought Pettson was crazy. But Findus didn't think so. Because after the old man climbed through the skylight in the attic, he found his fishing rod. Then he climbed back down, walked over to the well, and fished out the key. Then he opened the door to the shed and got out his tools and fixed the flat tire on the bicycle and rode to the store and bought flour and a new pair of overalls and then came back home and made a tasty cake for Findus.

Then they sat together in the garden, drinking coffee and eating cake and playing Viennese waltzes on the wind-up gramophone, just like they always did on Findus's birthday. Pettson wasn't so crazy after all, was he?

Pettson's Pancake Mix

Ingredients:

¾ cup milk

2 tablespoons white vinegar

1 cup flour

2 tablespoons sugar

½ teaspoon baking soda

½ teaspoon salt

1 teaspoon baking powder

2 tablespoons butter

1 egg

Directions:

- Pour the milk into a large bowl then add the vinegar. Set aside for 3 minutes.
- In a separate bowl, combine the flour, sugar, baking soda, salt, and baking powder.
- Add the melted butter and egg into the milk. Mix well.
- Pour the flour mixture into the wet ingredients and stir with a fork until smooth.
- Heat and oil a large skillet using medium heat.
- Pour ⅓ cupfuls of batter onto the skillet, and cook until bubbles appear on the surface. Flip and cook until browned on the other side.

Make a "pancake" cake!

Using 3 pancakes, top each with whipped cream then stack 'em up and add strawberries, bananas, or blueberries on top. Or simply serve with butter and syrup.

Be sure to check out the first three books in the series!

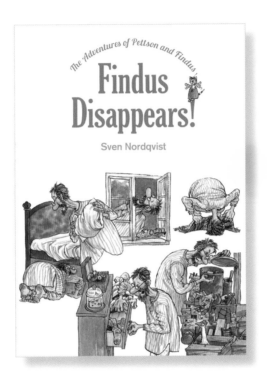

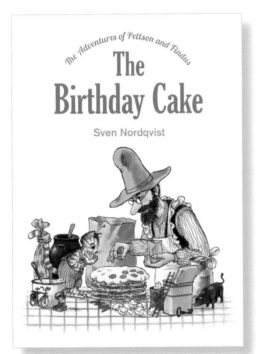

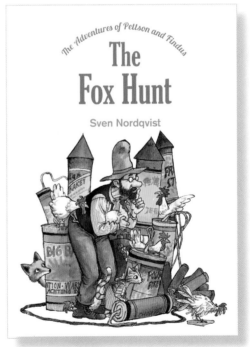

Sven Nordqvist is the author and illustrator who dreamed up this series. The beloved Pettson and Findus stories draw on Nordqvist's playful adventures with his two sons when they were younger. His unique illustrations are inspired by the delights of everyday life.

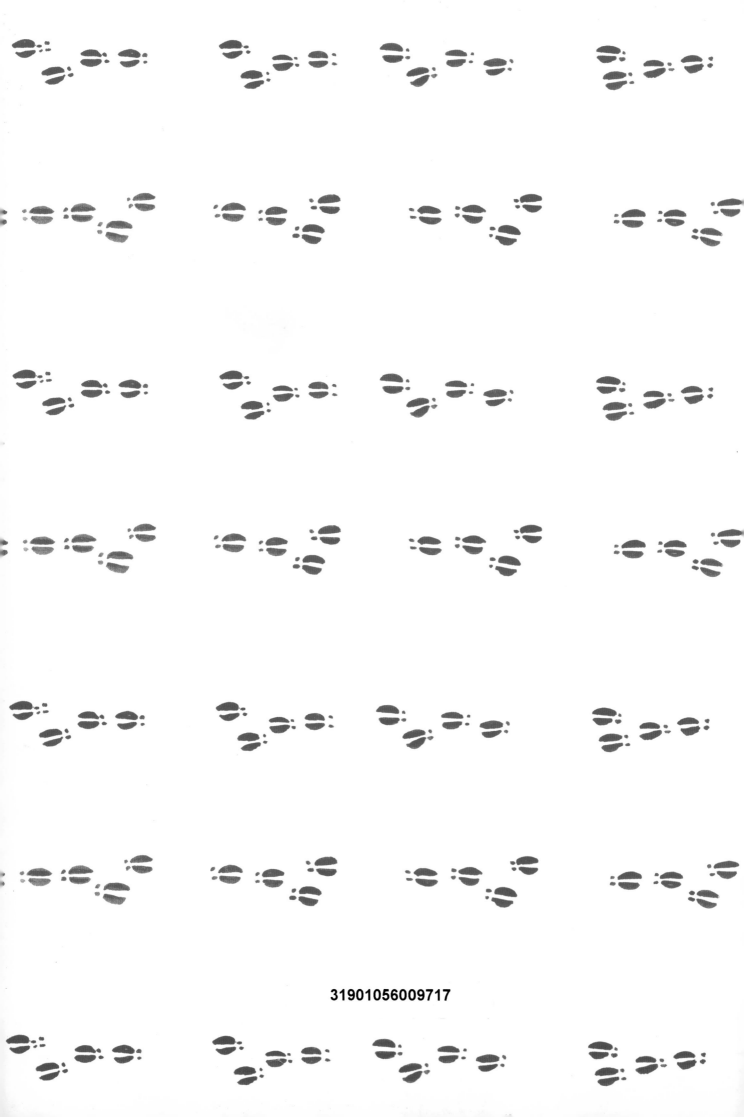